# The Crunching Munching Caterpillar

**tiger tales**
5 River Road, Suite 128, Wilton, CT 06897
This edition published in the United States 2019
First paperback edition (978-1-58925-403-9) published 2007
First hardcover edition (978-1-58925-025-3) published 2003
Originally published in Great Britain 2000
by Little Tiger Press Ltd.
Text copyright © 2000 Sheridan Cain
Illustrations copyright © 2000 Jack Tickle
ISBN-13: 978-1-68010-138-6
ISBN-10: 1-68010-138-2
Printed in China
LTP/1400/2377/0818

For more insight and activities,
visit us at www.tigertalesbooks.com

For my family
—S.C.

For Jim and Raechele
—J.T.

# The Crunching Munching Caterpillar

by Sheridan Cain

Illustrated by Jack Tickle

tiger tales

Caterpillar was always hungry.
For weeks he crunched and munched
his way through the fresh, juicy leaves
of a blackberry bush.

Bzzzzzzz

One day, Caterpillar was about to
crunch into another leaf when . . .

# Bzzzzzzzzzzzzz

Bumblebee landed beside him!

"Wow!" said Caterpillar.
"How did you get here?"
"Simple," said Bumblebee.
"I have wings. Look!"
"Oh, I'd like some of those,"
said Caterpillar.

Bumblebee flew up into the air and buzzed busily from flower to flower.

Bzzzzz

Bzzzz

"I'd love to fly like that," said Caterpillar.

"But you can't," said Bumblebee. "I have wings, and you have legs. Your legs are for walking."

"I guess so," sighed Caterpillar.

**Bzzzzzoommm**

Bumblebee flew off to the next bush. Watching Bumblebee fly had made Caterpillar *very* hungry, so he crunched and he munched until it was time for bed.

crunch munch
crunch munch
yaw-w-n!

Caterpillar woke to the sound of twittering. Birds swooped and soared in the early morning light.

Caterpillar was just about to start his breakfast when . . .

Sparrow landed
beside him.

"I'd love to fly high in the air like that," said Caterpillar.

"But you can't," said Sparrow. "You need to be as light as the dandelion fluff that floats on the breeze. You're much too big to fly. Your legs are for walking."

"I guess so," said Caterpillar sadly.

Caterpillar kept on crunching and munching all day and into the evening, when the sun began to set.

He wrapped a leaf around himself
to keep warm. He was just about to
go to sleep when . . .

Butterfly landed gracefully beside him.

"Oh, I wish I could fly like you," sighed Caterpillar. "But I'm too big, and I have legs instead of wings."

Butterfly smiled a secret, knowing smile. "Who knows? Maybe one day you will fly, light as a feather, like me," she said. "But now, little Caterpillar, you should go to sleep. You look very tired."

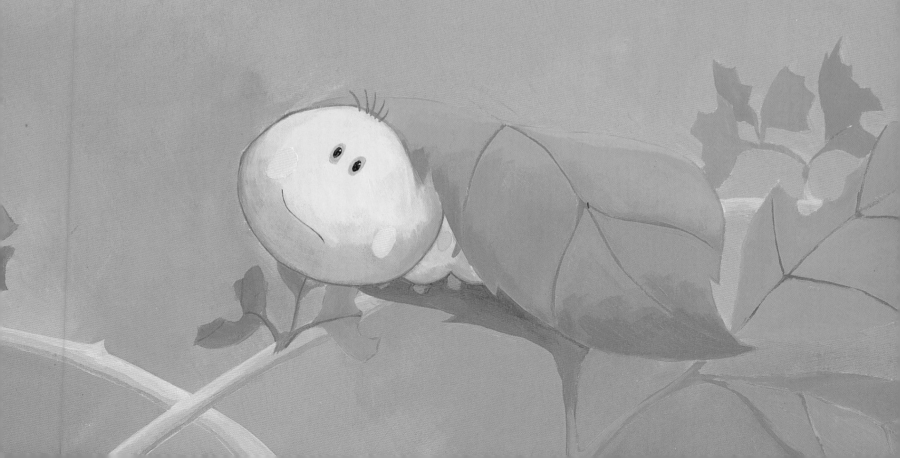

Butterfly was right. Caterpillar suddenly felt very sleepy.

As Butterfly flew off into the night sky, Caterpillar fell into a deep, deep sleep.

Caterpillar slept all through the winter, and his sleep was filled with dreams.

Zzzzzzzz Z Z Z z z z z z z z

He dreamed he had wings and

was soaring in the blue sky above the tall trees . . . .

He dreamed he was a piece of dandelion fluff, drifting toward the sun.

He dreamed he was as light as a feather,

floating on the breeze.

When Caterpillar woke up, he felt the warmth of the spring sun. He was stiff from his long sleep, but he did not feel very hungry. He stretched and stretched . . .

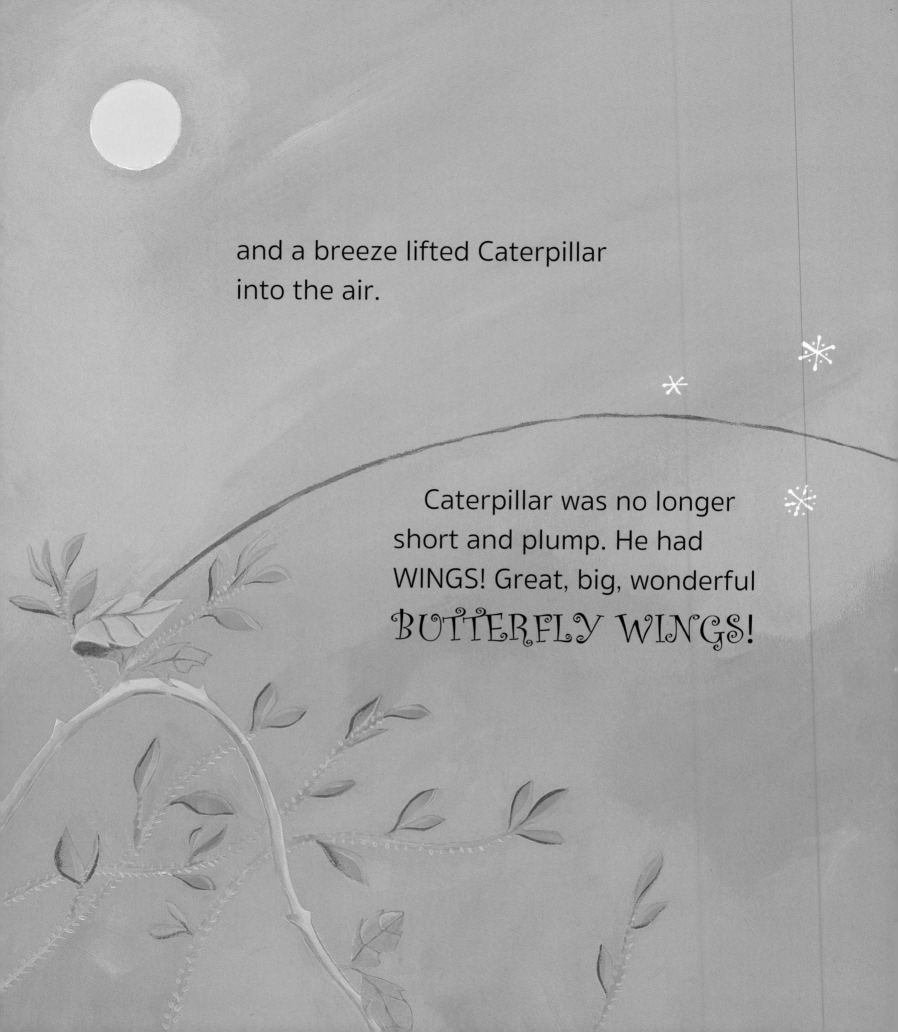

and a breeze lifted Caterpillar
into the air.

Caterpillar was no longer
short and plump. He had
WINGS! Great, big, wonderful
BUTTERFLY WINGS!

"Wow!" he said. "I'm flying! I'm really flying!"

## Sheridan Cain

Sheridan was born in London, where
she also went to school. She now lives in the
east of England. She is an avid gardener, and
the many small creatures who visit her
garden are an inspiration for
her children's books.

## Jack Tickle

Jack likes painting in acrylic because when
he spills coffee and food on his pictures, he can wipe
them clean again! He likes to eat gingerbread men
and chocolate cookies while he paints
and listens to loud guitar music.
Mr. Tickle lives in South West England
with his family and a large
cookie jar.